# nickythejazzcat

story and pictures by Carol Friedman

Baby cat Nicky

heard

# jazz

tunes one day.

He meowed to the music and

wished he could play!

He was wishing and hoping

he knew how to blow

when the coolest of jazz cats

came to wish him hello!

Hey baby NICKY

I'm so glad we could meet.

It's your trumpet pal ROY

I'll show you how to play sweet.

My friends call me "little jazz"

you'll be "little jazz cat"

ok little buddy?

What do you think about

that?

what do you

think about

that

little
cat?

ok **ROY**

can I sound just like you?

No way little jazz cat

your sound will be new!

You'll play with the best cats

they'll all come around

we'll show you some cool grooves

But you'll have your own

# sound!

So they jammed they got tight

they bebopped every night

this jazz cat learned

more every day.

Little Nicky got big

he was ready to gig

Roy said go jazz cat!

you're ready to

# play

Hi Nicky. It's **QUINCY**

my friends call me

# Q

Mumbles told me to call you

and Percy did too!

All the cats say you're the best in the land

so bring Dizzy, lets get busy,

will you play in my

# band?

that's what I'll do!

I'll give you a hand

and play in your band.

I'll play in your band

and it will be

# grand!

Hi Nicky. It's **LENA**

Thought I'd give you a ring.

Quincy just told me,

Lena this cat can swing!

The Duke loves you madly

and Basie does too.

Everyone's saying

I should

# sing

with you.

like

ella

and

sassy

and

billie

all

do!

too!

Hi NICKY It's GERRY

your old pal

# JERU

We're all jamming at my house

will you come and play too?

Miles and Gil will be there

so be there or be square...

we wrote a cool song just for you!

I'm no

square

i'll be

there

and

i'll

bring

my

**horn**

too

Hi Nicky. It's ABBEY

Will you play me your

# song?

Just show me the changes

and I'll sing along.

You're the real king of cats

you've got magic and

# style

your sound is so sweet

**Abbey dear Abbey**

**you make me smile too!**

# music

## is the magic

for me and for

# you

Hi Nicky. It's HAMP

You sure sound like a king.

Let's play Hamp's Boogie Woogie

and make the place

# swing!

We'll boogie and woogie

and jam 'til daylight

ok little jazz cat? It'll be

# dynamite!

hey
ba ba rebop
you're outta
sight!

ok Hamp

let's play

'til it's

light

**and**

**to**

**all**

**you**

**jazz**

**children**

have

a

# jazzy

good

night!

Thank you to Nicky's special friends

Roy Eldridge, Quincy Jones, Lena Horne, Gerry Mulligan,
Abbey Lincoln and Lionel Hampton.


and to his fans and admirers

Al and Linda, Michael, Amina, John, Nina, Tina, Marsha, Max, Bridget, Jerry, Bruce,
Mike, Lin, Allan, Debra, Marielle, Nick, Mark, Larry, Carol, Donna, Morna, Paul, Marlene,
Sally, Milt, Janis, Joseph, Jean, Harry, Joey, Deborah, Claudia, Ahmet, Teddy, Perry, Kevin,
Turid, Craig, Rufus, Walter, Vanessa, Cindy, Frank, Peter, Ellen, Lorraine, Ruth, Julie, Lynn,
David, Tom, Sylvia, Audre, Akiko, Howard, Irwin, Manny, Carin, Daniel, Ann, Fredda, Nia,
Monica, Johnny, Laura, Phil, Alfie, Ruby, Stella, Diana, Richard, Maria, Dennis, Steve,
Charlie, Mary, Scott, Pete, Alison, William, Anthony, Kenny, Bobby, Jeffrey and Gil.

My gratitude to Dr. Edwina Ho and to A.J. Collins


Through the years, I have known and photographed many jazz legends. My
cat Nicky and these great artists were fast friends. This book celebrates
their encounters and the spirit of art, music and improvisation.


Please visit our website to learn about jazz
music, products and programs for children.


www.nickythejazzcat.com

chick smack woody bunk andy king don bu
tiny gerald gil sy tadd swee'pea clare the la
sun ra monk fatha teddy eubie jelly roll fats t
sadik andrew sir roland the grey fox jumbo ja
jimmy cecil jess bill barry al erroll mal dick
george hootie ahmad ellis joe lou phineas
hank cow cow mary lou richie lennie oscar
mingus ray red rufus the judge paul reggie s
charles major buster benny tommy george
billy max phillie joe papa jo sid max leroy bo
jc connie arthur louis mickey dannie buddy
sam jack shadow ben mousie zutty klook p
lady day ella sassy mabel maxine etta ivie the
irene ina ray chippie lee shirley betty blossom
annie pinky june nancy chris beverly ethel bess
mr. b johnny joe muddy babs king pleasure f